# A JUST ONE MORE BOOK
## Just For You

# Baby Koala
# Finds a Home

by Valerie Tripp

Illustrated by Sandra Cox Kalthoff

Developed by The Hampton-Brown Company, Inc.

**CHILDRENS PRESS** ®

**CHICAGO**

# Word List

Give children books they can read by themselves, and they'll always ask for JUST ONE MORE. This book is written with 85 of the most basic words in our language, all repeated in an appealing rhythm and rhyme.

| | | | |
|---|---|---|---|
| a | get | me | snake |
| above | go | more | so |
| all | good | morning | sorry |
| and | great | mother | stay |
| another | green | mouse | surprise(d) |
| are | | my | |
| away | have | | tea |
| | head | nice | that |
| baby | her | no | the |
| be | here('s) | now | their |
| bed | his | | them |
| best | home | off | then |
| big(gest) | | old | there |
| | I('m) | on | they('ve) |
| can('t) | is | one | this |
| | its | open | to |
| day | | other | top |
| | just | our | tree |
| eat | | owl | |
| ever | koala | | up |
| eyes | | place | |
| | leaves | please | very |
| find(s) | like | pop(s) | |
| found | little | | when |
| from | long | see | |
| | look | seen | you |
| | | sleep | |

**Library of Congress Cataloging-in-Publication Data**

Tripp, Valerie, 1951-
  Baby Koala finds a home.

  (A Just one more book just for you)
  Summary: A baby koala and her mother try to find an unoccupied branch in a eucalyptus tree.
  [1. Koalas—Fiction.  2. Stories in rhyme]
I. Kalthoff, Sandra Cox, ill.    II. Title.
III.  Series.
PZ8.3.T698Bab   1987       [E]       87-6325
ISBN 0-516-01577-X

2 3 4 5 6 7 8 9 10 R 92 91 90 89

CHILDRENS PRESS, Chicago
Copyright ©1987 by Regensteiner
Publishing Enterprises, Inc. All
rights reserved. Published
simultaneously in Canada. Printed
in the United States of America.

Baby Koala
and her mother
go from one tree
to another.

They look and look.
They look all day
to find a place
where they can stay.

On . . . and on . . . and on
they go
to find a tree
to be their home.

Now here's a tree!
Its leaves are sweet,
just the kind
koalas eat.

But when the koalas
go to bed,
a little mouse
pops up her head.

I'm sorry, koalas.
You can't stay.
This is MY branch.
Please go away.

So Baby Koala
and her mother
go from that branch
to another.

Now here's a branch!
Its leaves are sweet,
just the kind
koalas eat.

But when the koalas
go to bed,
a big, old owl
pops up his head.

I'm sorry, koalas.
You can't stay.
Get OFF my branch!
Now go away.

So Baby Koala
and her mother
go from that branch
to another.

Now here's a branch!
Its leaves are sweet,
just the kind
koalas eat.

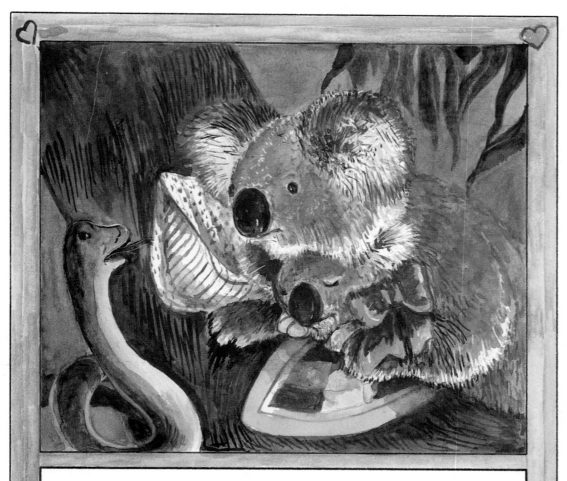

But when the koalas
go to bed,
a long, green snake
pops up his head.

No, no, koalas!
You can't stay.
Get OFF my branch.
GO!  Get away!

So Baby Koala
and her mother
go from that branch
to another.

**JUST ONE MORE** branch
is on the tree,
just one more place
for them to be.

So, Baby Koala
and her mother
sleep on that branch
and no other.

Good morning!   Good morning!
When they open their eyes,
the koalas see
a **GREAT** surprise!

The very top branch
is nice and green,
the biggest branch
they've EVER seen!

Then up pop mouse
and owl and snake.
They are surprised.
The branch is GREAT!

We LIKE this place
at the top of the tree.
Can I stay here?
And me? and ME?

This is OUR branch!
Pop up and see.
You can't STAY here,
but come for tea!